This book belongs to

Rosie

....

First published in 2014 by Miles Kelly Publishing Ltd
Harding's Barn, Bardfield End Green, Thaxted, Essex, CM6 3PX, UK

2 4 6 8 10 9 7 5 3 1

Publishing Director Belinda Gallagher
Creative Director Jo Cowan
Editor Fran Bromage
Senior Designer Joe Jones
Production Manager Elizabeth Collins
Reprographics Stephan Davis, Jennifer Hunt, Thom Allaway

ISBN 978-1-78209-489-0

Printed in China

British Library Cataloguing-in-Publication Data
A catalogue record for this book is available from the British Library

ACKNOWLEDGEMENTS

The publishers would like to thank the following artists
who have contributed to this book:

Cover (main): Estelle Corke at Advocate Art
Insides: Elizabeth Sawyer

Made with paper from a sustainable forest

www.mileskelly.net   info@mileskelly.net

Jack and the Beanstalk

Miles Kelly

This is the story of how Jack did a silly thing, but all was well in the end.

Jack and his mother were very poor, and one day Jack's

Jack and the Beanstalk

mother told him to take their only cow to market, and sell her for as much money as he could possibly get.

On the way to market, Jack met a funny little man who offered him five magic beans in exchange for the cow.

Jack should have realized
that this was rather odd,
but he took
the beans,
handed

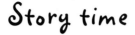

over the cow and ran home.
Jack's mother was so
furious she flung the beans
out of the window and sent
Jack straight to bed.

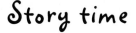

Story time

The next morning, Jack wandered outside to find his mother staring in amazement at an enormous beanstalk. It reached right up into the clouds. "I told you they were magic beans," said Jack, and he began to climb.

Jack and the Beanstalk

Jack climbed and climbed. At the top of the beanstalk was a huge castle. Jack knocked on the door, and a gigantic woman opened it. "My husband eats boys for breakfast," she said. Before Jack could reply, the ground

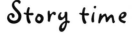

started to shake, so she hid Jack in a cupboard.

A colossal man stumped into the kitchen. "Fee fi fo fum! I smell the blood of an Englishman!" he roared.

"Don't be silly, dear. You can smell the eggs I've

cooked," said the giant's wife.

The giant gobbled up the whole pile of eggs. Then, he poured a bag of gold onto the table, counted all the coins and fell asleep.

Jack darted out of the cupboard, grabbed the bag

of gold and slithered down the beanstalk as fast as he could. Jack's mother was astonished when she saw the gold. They bought two new cows and

12

plenty of food to eat.

But after a time, Jack decided to climb the beanstalk again. The giant's wife wasn't very pleased to see him. "We lost a bag of gold the last time you were here," she growled.

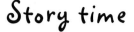

Then the ground began to shake and tremble. Jack ran and hid in the cupboard.

"Fee fi fo fum! I smell the blood of an Englishman!" the giant roared.

"Don't be silly, dear. You can smell the chickens I've

cooked," said the giant's wife, handing him a plate.

The giant gobbled the lot. Then he lifted a tiny white goose onto the table. "Lay!" he commanded, and the goose laid a golden egg. With a smile, the giant fell asleep.

Jack darted out of the cupboard, grabbed the goose and slid down the beanstalk. Jack's mother was amazed when she saw the golden eggs. This time they bought a whole herd of cows.

After a while, Jack climbed

Jack and the Beanstalk

the beanstalk again. The giant's wife looked very cross. "We lost a golden goose the last time you were here," she growled. Then the ground began to shake. This time Jack hid in a drawer.

"Fee fi fo fum! I smell the

blood of an Englishman!"
roared the giant.

"Try the cupboard," said
the giant's wife, but Jack
wasn't in the cupboard.

"Well, eat your breakfast,"
said the giant's wife, handing
him a plate of sausages. The

Jack and the Beanstalk

giant ate the lot, then he lifted a harp onto the table. "Play!" he commanded. The harp played so sweetly that the giant was soon asleep.

Jack crept out from the drawer and grabbed the golden harp. But the harp

Jack and the Beanstalk

stopped playing when Jack touched it. The giant woke up with a start and ran after Jack, who climbed down the beanstalk as fast he could, still carrying the harp.

As soon as Jack reached the ground he ran to fetch

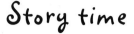
an axe and called for his
mother. Together they
chopped through the giant
beanstalk. Down tumbled the
huge beanstalk, and down
tumbled the giant. And that
was the end of him!

So, Jack and his mother

lived happily for the rest of their days with a whole herd of cows, the little white goose and the golden harp.

The End